PETER AND THE SKELETON PIRATE

Minecraft Fairy Tale Series

By: Tom Garzan, Brayden Bush
& Z. Willingham

TABLE OF CONTENTS

INTRODUCTION

Welcome to the Minecraft Fairy Tales

Series! Through these books you will

explore the classic tales – with a twist. A

Minecraft twist! Travel through the world of

fantasy with these tales that will captivate

you until the end!

PART ONE

Second Star on the Left

The night was bright and clear with a full shining moon when Peter and Tink flew from the windowsill of the Darling house. Wendy and her brothers were waving at the pair, almost falling out of the window themselves.

"What a great party, Tink!" Peter said.

"Yes, Peter. That was the best. I always love visiting our friends," Tink replied.

The pair had spent the night at the Darling house, playing and eating sweets all night long. They had played many different games like tag, board games like Mouse Trap and Monopoly, and had to catch Peter's shadow, as it kept getting away. Wendy sewed it back on as tight as she could, hoping that it would not get loose – again – anytime soon.

Peter and Tink left as the sun was coming up over the city of London, heading back to Neverland and their comfortable beds to sleep the day away after a great night. Tink was already nodding off next to Peter.

"Tink, you can sleep on my shoulder for the way home if you want." "Oh, thank you, Peter. I really am tired and should rest. Are you sure you can navigate the way home?"

"Of course I can!"

Tink climbed onto Peter's shoulder and started to snore next to his ear. He was confident that he could find the right way home. He knew it was the second star on the right. That had always been the way to Neverland.

Peter flew higher in the air, Tink asleep on his shoulder. Once he had gotten high enough, he saw that the sun was rising too quickly and he needed to get to the star right away or he would miss his chance to go home and they would have to wait until the next night when the stars came out again.

Looking at the stars, Peter saw there were four, two on either side of the quickly lowering moon. For a minute, he thought he there was something in his eye, but no, there were definitely four stars up there.

"Well, which is the correct one?" said Peter aloud. He had never seen four stars before; it had always been just two so he never had to guess which one was the correct one.

"Now which one is on the right?" Peter was confused as to which his left was and which his right was. Looking closely, he saw that he did not have much more time to decide. The sky was starting to lighten fast and he would have to make a decision soon or be stuck in the Real World another day.

"I think it's that one. Yes, definitely that one. It has to be. I've flown home a million times, so I know this." Peter was confident that he was choosing the second star on the right and flew towards it quickly, trying to outrun the sun.

He had just made it and started to enter the portal that would take them to Neverland when things started to get…weird.

All of a sudden, he could feel himself and Tink being pulled into this strange swirling vortex with bright colors and flashes of light. He felt his body being yanked at, as if someone was trying to change his shape.

Tink woke up on his shoulder and yelled, "Peter! What is happening? Where are we?" Her voice could barely be heard over the loud sucking noises coming from the portal they were falling through.

All of a sudden, there was a *pop* and Peter looked down to see his body had turned square! Glancing over, he saw that Tink's body had changed shape as well.

What kind of magic was this? It was unlike anything Peter had encountered in Neverland before. Peter worried that maybe he had chosen the wrong star and that they were falling into a world unknown to them.

After another minute or two, they both crashed down into a bright blue sky with fluffy yet square clouds all around. Peter looked down to see water below them.

Tink started to scream and they realized they were no longer flying. They definitely weren't in Neverland, Peter was sure of that now.

A moment later they crashed down, hard, on a wooden surface. The breath was knocked out of Peter and Tink was in a daze beside him. Looking around, they saw they were on the deck of a pirate ship, surrounded by menacing looking pirates.

"Where in the world have you taken us, Peter?"

PART TWO

Captain Boney and the Skeleton Crew

Surrounded by the crew, Peter took in the fierce looking pirates. They looked to be skeletons covered in…dirty socks? *No that can't be right. What kind of pirate is a skeleton? In addition, one who wears clothing made of dirty socks. I must be dreaming,* Peter thought.

Each pirate had a shirt and a pair of pants. Some even had shoes that were made out of many layers of socks. In addition, all were so filthy and smelled so badly that Peter had to lean back from the stench. Of course, that did not help, as there were pirates circled behind him as well.

The ship itself was a typical pirate ship, though everything was dirtier than normal. It looked as though it was deliberately made that way, though, and not a matter of chance. Looking up, there was a large flag that had a red background with a bright multicolored dirty sock on it. How strange, indeed.

"Well, well. What do we have here?" said a voice that was as crusty as the clothing on the pirate it came from.

He was obviously the captain. Covered in dirty sock clothing and sporting a peg leg, a hook for a hand, an eye patch over one eye – though no eyeball in the other. He wore an outfit consisting of green pants, a red coat, striped shirt and a black pirate hat. He looked like a typical pirate – except for being a skeleton covered in socks, of course.

"Where are we?" Peter asked, standing up and putting Tink on his shoulder. He had gotten them into this mess and he was determined to get them out of it.

"Why are you stowaways on my ship?"

"Ship? What ship is this?" Tink had her hands on her hips, her face red with anger at the implication that they had snuck onto the ship. Sure, they had done it tons of times with the Jolly Roger, but this captain was no Hook and they definitely did not come here on purpose.

The crusty captain leaned closer and inspected the tiny Tink. He leaned in so close that Tink had to wave her hand in front of her face to get rid of the smell of his breath. She thought she might faint from the stench.

"This here, little miss, is the Stinky Sock. The scariest – and smelliest – pirate ship in the Overworld. And who might you be?" His voice sounded like he had swallowed a toad and was croaking all his words out.

Tink crossed her arms and looked away, while Peter said, "I'm Peter and this is Tink. We were meant to go to our home in

Neverland, but apparently, we went to the wrong star."

"WE! Peter Pan, you take that back! I was asleep. It was YOU who took us here!" Tink was furious at Peter for including her in an escapade that had not only stopped them from getting home, but had changed their shape and landed them in the midst of a pirate ship filled with crazy looking pirates.

"Sounds like that little lady there doesn't think you should have come here. I'm inclined to agree, since you be invading my pirate ship without me permission."

Peter started to feel the instant dislike in the air as the pirates shuffled closer to them. "And who are you, fine captain?"

"My name be Captain Boney. My full name is Dirty B. Hind, the B stands for Boney." Captain Boney seemed very proud of his name and Peter tried to hold in his laugh. Tink was not so lucky and let out a huge laugh for such a tiny little fairy.

"Are you laughing at me? How dare you! I'll teach you to laugh at Captain Boney. Mocksocks get them!" Captain Boney pointed his boney finger at Peter and

Tink and the group of sock-covered pirates got ready to lunge at them.

Just as they were about to jump, Tink sprinkled dust on her and Peter in a fit of fright. "Peter, FLY!"

Taking a chance and jumping as high as he could, Peter and Tink flew into the air, high above the pirate ship. They looked down to see that the pirates had all fallen upon each other and were stuck on each other's bones like a big pile of pretzels.

PART THREE
Village of the Missing

Now that they were free from the current danger – and could fly again – Peter and Tink flew high in the air away from the ship, trying to find a safe place to land.

Flying for a while, they started to see the land turn from water to green grassy areas with trees and bushes. There were even beautiful blue lakes. Everything was square, though.

"What is this strange world you brought us to, Peter?" Tink was still annoyed at being turned square. In addition, being captured by pirates did not help her mood.

"I'm sorry, Tink. I really thought I knew the way to get home, but when I looked up, there were four stars in the sky, not two like always. I got confused between my left and my right since I've never had to use them before." Peter was sorry that he had landed them in this mess. However, on the other hand, he was excited about a new adventure. Sure, Neverland was fun, but he rarely got to travel to anywhere but there or the Real World to visit Wendy and her brothers. This was a place he had never even thought of before and he hoped once they were safe, maybe they could come back again.

"Well, you better get us home Peter Pan, or I'll never forgive you!"

"Easy, Tink. I can do this. It is just like fighting Hook at home. We just need to find a way to get through the day and then at night, when the stars are back up, we can fly home safely."

Tink huffed and then started to fly lower, trying to get a better view of the ground. "Look, Peter, there is a village there. Perhaps they can help us?"

"Great idea, Tink!" Peter was glad for her awesome fairy eyesight and they started to sink lower to the ground.

Just as they landed, they saw these huge metal beasts lumbering in front of them. They were as tall as the trees and completely square. Covered in tan metal with red eyes, they looked super scary.

"Stay close, Tink. This doesn't seem to be any friendlier than the pirate ship." Peter pushed Tink so she was up on his shoulder behind his neck.

The metal giants came closer, their fists at the ready. "Who are you? What are you doing on our land?"

"Whoa there, metal dude. I am Peter and I am just here for a safe place to hang out until nightfall. I already encountered the pirates and I don't want any trouble, okay?"

"Pirates, eh? And what did the pirates do to you?" The one who appeared to be the leader had stepped forward to ask the questions.

"The stinky buggers circled us on their ship and tried to jump us, but we managed to fly away."

"Us? I thought you said it was just you?" The leader raised a metal eyebrow at Peter.

"Oh, darn. Ok, yeah, it is not just me. Tink, come out." Tink came around to stand on Peter's shoulder and crossed her arms.

"This is Tink. She is a fairy from our world, Neverland. Look, I took the wrong star from the Real World and we landed here in your strange square world. We just need a place to hide until nightfall when the stars come back out and we can fly home. Please?"

"It's not up to me. Take them to the village, boys." He turned to Peter and Tink saying, "Come quietly and you won't be harmed."

Tink leaned over to whisper in Peter's ear, "Just do it, Peter. We are in enough trouble." Peter nodded and they walked towards the small village of houses surrounded by the metal beasts.

The village was comprised of several houses, all made out of square blocks. There looked to be a school and a restaurant, too. Many people were looking out their windows as the group passed by. Parents reached for their children and pulled them close in fear of the two strange beings the metal giants escorted through town.

They were lead to what looked like the biggest house in the village. It was made of red brick with brown doors and small windows on either side. *At least there would be a way to get out once we get inside,* thought Peter.

Inside there was a man sitting at a table. He had a square body – of course – brown hair and green eyes. He looked to be about forty years old and he was *huge.* Almost as big as the metal beasts, but definitely human. He was wearing a clean red shirt that looked to be covered in sawdust.

"What have we here, Tram?" asked the man while he sat eating at the table. The spoon didn't stop its up and down movement, even when he talked. The man sure seemed to like his food and nothing, not even two strange beings in his village, looked to stop him from eating.

"They were found right outside the village, sir. I was not sure who they are or what their purpose is. They claim they are from another world and here by mistake." The metal beast paused. "They said they met with the Mocksocks, sir."

This made the man pause from his meal. "Oh, really?" He turned to fully look at Peter and Tink now. "So, you've met with our dear Captain Boney, have you?"

"Dear Captain Boney?" Tink was annoyed again. Her light grew brighter when she was angry and her voice came out with a tinkling noise that hurt the other's ears. "That pirate is a disgrace and someone should do something about him!"

"I'm glad to hear you share my opinion then. I am Benjamin Wood haul, but you can call me Ben. I am the wood hauler of this village and everyone comes to me thinking I can help solve their problems. Who might you be?"

"I'm Peter and this here is Tink. We come from Neverland and seemed to have made a mistake in which star to head to go home. We fell into this world and landed on a pirate ship that the captain called the Stinky Sock. We are just looking for a place to stay until it gets dark and the stars come out. Then Tink can show us the way home." Peter took a deep breath after saying all that without stopping.

"Fly home? You mean you can fly?" Ben seemed skeptical.

"Well, yeah. Tink is a fairy and she has fairy dust." Peter gave Ben a look that said *duh.*

Ben gave Peter an appraising look. "Well, that is something that will come in mighty handy, Peter. Tram here," he gestured to the metal giant, "and the other iron golems, along with all us villagers, have been trying to get out from under Captain Boney's thumb for a while now. He keeps capturing our people and turning them into skeletons to serve on his crew. We have been planning a raid soon. Would you and the little miss be willing to help us?" Peter was shocked by this revelation and knew he had seen the same type of true evil in his own pirate villain in Neverland.

"Wow, Ben. I had no idea. We would be happy to stay and help you today until we have to leave. We have our own pirate troubles in Neverland and know what it is like to have a villain in the midst."

Ben looked truly thankful and when Peter glanced at the iron golems – now that

he knew what the metal beasts were called –
he saw they seemed impressed by him
stepping up to help them.

"He has taken half our village for his
crew so far, including my wife and
daughter." Ben looked devastated at that
statement. "He keeps taking our socks on
top of it all. All the people left in the village
keep getting colds from having to go out
with no socks on. I am determined to get my
family back. I have a plan to take him
down."

Ben invited Peter and Tink to sit at the table and offered them plates of stew and some spoons. When Ben saw how little Tink was, he went and found a small thimble that Tink could use as a cup to drink her stew from. She was touched that he went to this trouble. Peter and Tink dug in right away. They were both starving because they had not eaten since the party the night before, and it was already midday here.

"Come tonight, we will have Captain Boney at our mercy and all our family will be turned back from Mocksocks into themselves!" Ben was cheering the idea of finally getting his wife and daughter back.

PART FOUR

Attack on the Dirty Sock

"So, what's the plan, Ben?" Peter asked between slurps.

"Captain Boney has a certain magic that he uses to control the Mocksocks. The magic comes from his peg leg and his hook hand. If we can find a way to get both those items away from him, then the Mocksocks should turn back into themselves and be free to come home." Ben seemed like he had it all planned out.

"But how do we get them away from Captain Boney?" Tink asked, daintily letting out a burp.

"I figure we can have my crew here," Ben pointed to the iron golems, "and a group of the villagers take on the Mocksocks on the deck and restrain them. If you and Tink can fly into Boney's window while he is asleep and take his hook and peg leg, then we can have everyone transform back to themselves immediately."

"Genius!" yelled Tram from the other side of the room.

Ben smiled at him and the other iron golems who had gathered around the fire to discuss their plan of action. They were stronger than the other villagers and would be key in helping keep the Mocksocks contained and calm until they transformed back. Ben did not want them hurt as they were his friends...they just did not remember that since they had been turned into skeletons.

"I say we go once it starts to get a little darker," said Tink. "I can sprinkle Peter and we should be able to fly easily and not be detected. If your villagers swim to the outside of the ship and you have your iron golems waiting on land by the ramp leading up to the ship, then we can do this all at once."

"Excellent plan, my dear little miss," said Ben with a smile on his face. "My daughter is going to love meeting such a brave fairy."

Tink blushed at the compliment.

***

Later that night, once everyone was in position, Tink sprinkled Peter with dust and they both took off in the air. They flew high over the ship to make sure everyone was where they should be. The plan was ready to be implemented.

Peter could see Ben with about twenty villagers all lined up in the water along the dark side of the ship. Once Tram and his iron golem crew were able to get on the boat, they would lower a rope ladder to help them climb.

Peter and Tink could see the iron golems hiding behind the bushes just steps away from the ramp up to the ship. Flying a bit lower, Tink shone brightly to give the alert to both sets of waiting rescuers that it was time to start.

They watched anxiously from the highest sail as Tram and his brothers crept out from behind the bushes and moved slowly up the ramp. They had oiled all their moving pieces earlier to make sure none of them creaked and alerted anyone too soon.

As soon as they made it onto the ship, they saw that no one was around. It seemed like all the Mocksocks were down below decks. Tram quickly moved to lower the ladder and Tink and Peter watched as the villagers climbed up onto the deck one by one.

Once everyone was up, they waved to Tink and Peter and headed towards the stairs leading below. It was up to them now to secure the Mocksocks while Peter went in to try to get Captain Boney's magical peg leg and hook.

***

The villagers and iron golems snuck below deck in a single-file line. They tried to make as little sound as possible to not alert their quarry of their presence. Once they had reached the below decks, they saw something that surprised them and stopped them in their tracks.

The Mocksocks were all in their hammocks, sewing and singing. The song they sung went, *"Socks we sew, so our bones won't grow. Yo ho, yo ho, a skeleton's life for me."*

Each one of them had a pile of socks next to them and they were bent over sewing them all together into clothing. Looking closely, Ben could see one of the Mocksocks was sewing what looked like his own socks and that Mocksock appeared it be...crying? It dawned on him a minute later that this must be his wife!

He turned and whispered, "I think they will know us! I do not think they will fight.

Everyone, quickly and quietly take off your hoods and show your faces!"

As soon as they had all done that, Ben stepped forward into the light given off by the lanterns and showed his face. The one who had been sewing his dirty socks together dropped the socks and gasped as only a skeleton could.

Though she did not have eyes, the Mocksock Ben thought was his wife started wailing and crying. He rushed over to shush her as he saw other Mocksocks dropping their sewing and rushing to their loved ones.

Ben realized this was not a fight. It was a rescue! He only hoped that Peter and Tink could come through and save all these people turned Mocksocks.

***

Peter and Tink slowly flew lower and landed on the upper deck. After checking to make sure no one was around, they both flew up and over the side and peeked into the windows of Captain Boney's cabin.

There was a single lantern lit and it looked like the skeleton captain was fast asleep in his hammock. Unfortunately, his peg leg and hook were still attached to him. This was not going to be an easy task, but the villagers were counting on them, so they could not let them down.

Creeping into the window, Peter told Tink to stand on top of a dresser and keep an eye out the door for anyone coming. He crossed the floor, flying slightly above the wood boards to avoid making them creak and waking Captain Boney.

As Peter got closer, he could smell the captain's breath. Oh, man did it stink! He did not get the name Stinky Sock for his ship for just smelly socks, that is for sure! He slowly reached out to grab ahold of the peg leg, hoping it would come off easily.

After giving it a light tug, he found out it was firmly attached. Oh no, what was he going to do now? Peter glanced back at Tink to make sure she was all right. Just as he looked back, he saw that Captain Boney's skeleton eye was wide open.

Peter froze in fear.

"Trying to take me leg and hook, were you? You have been talking to the wrong people, Peter. You won't get them that easily!"

Boney jumped out of his hammock and grabbed his sword. It was a pirate's cutlass and it was sharp enough that it could cut through a full salad's worth of vegetables in one stroke.

PART FIVE

The Villager's Revenge

"I won't let you do this to the villagers anymore, Boney. We have a way of taking care of evil pirates like you in Neverland!"

Peter jumped back and pulled out his own short sword out from its scabbard at his waist. Though it was not as sharp as Captain Boney's was, it was filled with Neverland magic that could take on any pirate captain in any world.

The two started to battle, sword to sword. Ringing and clashing could be heard all over the ship. From the below, the villagers and Mocksocks listened to the battle above that would win or lose them their freedom. All knew that if Peter and Tink did not win, then they would all be turned into Mocksocks and never be saved again.

Peter lunged and was able to knock Boney into a table and make him lose his balance. He went in to knock the pirate captain down to the ground where he could pull of Boney's peg leg, but the old skeleton pirate was too quick for him, jumping to his feet and meeting Peter's sword swing in a crash of metal against metal.

"You won't win, Boney! I've got goodness backing me!" Peter shouted at the captain, trying to reason with him. "If you just give up your peg leg and hook now, the villagers and we will let you go free to live your life as you please, providing you promise never to imprison anyone again. It's a fair offer."

"NEVER! This is my ship, this is my world and I will be the greatest captain alive! I will enslave the whole Overworld as skeletons and make myself king! I will have a whole slew of ships and skeleton crews to serve my every desire. You cannot stop me, Peter. You and your little tiny brat of a fairy won't stop me!" Boney was angry now and lashed out, knocking Peter's sword from his hand and making him fall back into a corner.

With no sword and no way out of the corner as the evil skeleton captain advanced toward him, sword out, Peter was trapped.

He thought it was the end and closed his eyes, waiting for the blow that would end all hope for the villagers and Mocksocks below.

Tink would not let that happen, not to her Peter! She flew toward Boney and started to fly around his head, blinking in his eyes to try to make him lose his concentration so Peter could get away.

All that did was make Boney angrier, though. He swatted at Tink, like a bug, and she flew into the wall above Peter's head.

Then something amazing happened.

When Boney had swatted Tink, she had dropped some of her dust onto his leg by accident.

Boney's peg leg started to float in the air!

All three watched in amazement as the wooden leg floated high above their heads, well beyond Captain Boney's reach. High enough it could only be reached by someone super tall – or someone who could fly.

"Hey! What are you doing with me leg?" Boney yelled in fright.

"That's right, Boney," Peter mocked the skeleton who was having trouble standing now that he was without his other leg. "Tink, quick! Get the hook!"

Tink fluttered over, well out of Boney's reach, and sprinkled some fairy dust onto his hook. At once, it started to float in the air just as the peg leg had.

"No, no, no! You cannot do this! You cannot do this to me. I was going to be a king. I was going to rule the world!" Boney fell to the wooden floor, sobbing like a child who had lost his favorite toys.

Peter shook his head and put his sword back in his scabbard. "You will never win against good, Boney. Bad never wins. You are no longer a captain. Go home to the Netherworld where you can be with other monsters like you. If you ever set foot in the Overworld again, I will come back and we will capture you. Understand?"

Boney sobbed harder, but between the crying, they saw him nod and heard him say, "Yes, Peter." He knew he was done and there was nothing left for him but to take the offer and escape to the Netherworld.

"Good."

Peter flew up, grabbed the peg leg hook where they floated, and tucked them into his shirt. Opening the door, Peter and Tink climbed up the steps to the top deck and saw a cheering group of villagers. Many were covered in dirty socks.

"Ben, what's going on?" Peter asked as soon as he had spotted the villager.

"You did it, Peter and Tink! You helped us save our families. Once you took Boney's peg leg and hook, everyone turned back to normal. Look! This is my wife,

Lucy, and my daughter, Susie." Ben put his arms around an older woman and a young girl who were both dressed in dirty socks. His eyes were shining with unshed tears at having his family back.

"WE did it, Ben. I am so glad you guys all have your families back. Boney is in his room, sobbing. I don't think you will have any trouble from him anytime soon."

Tink flew over to sit on the little girl's shoulder. "Hi, Susie. I'm Tink. Your father has said such nice things about you and I hope we can be friends."

Peter and Ben smiled as the young girl and Tink chatted away. It was time to gather everyone up and head on home to his or her village. Tink had one last surprise in store for them all.

Clapping her hands, she had Ben get everyone to quiet down and give her their attention. "Hello, all! You have had quite an ordeal and to make it easier to get back home, I have decided to help you all. Please hold still, this will just take a minute."

Tink flew above everyone and golden fairy dust sprinkled down from the sky, coating them all in a glowing mist.

"Now, all you need to do is think happy thoughts, and we can fly home." Tink smiled down at everyone.

At once, people started to rise up. The whole group of fifty or so people, including five iron golems, all rose in the air. They were amazed and many were laughing in pure delight.

Peter took the lead and with Ben, he led them all back home to safety and their village, never to see – or smell – a stinky dirty sock again.

PART SIX

Happily Ever After

A month had passed since Peter and Tink's adventure in the Overworld. As promised, they came back to the village to see their friends. Finding the right star now came easily to Peter once he had learned to tell his right from his left. Apparently, your left hand made an L shape when you stuck your index finger up and your thumb out. Who knew?

They returned to a celebration!

Everyone was smiling and laughing. Many were dancing and there was tons of food on tables all around the village square. Even the animals were running around, happy that their masters had returned happy and healthy.

Ben had been made Head Person of the village and was responsible for dispensing justice and seeing to the safety of everyone. Peter and Tink could not think of anyone more suited for the job. He still went out, cut, and hauled wood daily – and his shirt was still covered in sawdust.

Once everyone had had his or her fill of food, Ben presented Peter and Tink each with a medal made from Glowstone, a special type of gem only found in the Overworld. He even made sure to have a tiny one for Tink. She was overjoyed and rushed over to show Susie. They had become great friends since the night of rescuing.

Tram, the leader of the iron golems, had been given the task of seeing to Boney's ship. He made sure that it was taken apart and used to build new houses for the villagers. He was then sent to any neighboring towns to make sure no one else had need of protection now that Boney had lost his power.

Boney had not been heard from since, but there were reports of people seeing him cross the portal into the Netherworld. Peter knew he might be back one day, but he counted on Ben, Tram and the villagers to know how to take care of him. Ben kept the peg leg and hook in a locked chest that only he had the key to.

After a fun filled day, Peter and Tink knew it was time to return home. Tink sprinkled Peter with fairy dust and they rose into the air, waving at all their friends. All the villagers turned out to wave goodbye to their brave rescuers. Peter and Tink knew they had made friends for life.

Just as they had gotten high enough in the sky, Peter turned to Tink and said, "I think you should navigate this time, Tink. It did not turn out so well last time for me.

Nevertheless, WOW! What an adventure we had!"

The End

ABOUT THE AUTHORS

Tom Garzan

Tom Garzan loves all things Minecraft and fairy tales. At his children's urging, he combined his love of both into this exciting new series. He currently lives in the Northeastern U.S. with his 5 children, wife, 2 dogs, 14 chickens, 2 rabbits, a goat and a rather rude pig. He is excited to bring you a whole new way of reading fairy tales!

Facebook:

https://www.facebook.com/authortomgarzan

/

Find free audio versions on the Minecraft Fairy Tales YouTube Channel:

https://www.youtube.com/channel/UC5qza

K3sw1Gbor3kcEkT2LA

Z. Willingham

Z. Willingham is a seventh grader with a passion for Minecraft and reading. He plays it daily, much to his mother's insanity. Now becoming a teenager, he has decided it is time to go to work and help his friend, Tom Garzan, to write these awesome Minecraft stories.

Brayden Bush

B.T. Bush is a third grader with a love for video games and books. Learning multiplication by day and dreaming of Minecraft by night, he is also just learning to play the guitar. He also helps his friend, Tom Garzan, come up with new and exciting tales to share with the world.

Other Books in the Series

Steve and the Seven Iron Golems

Steve is a prince who has a charmed life, but when his father dies, his mother is forced to marry the evil Duke Herobrine. Herobrine takes over the kingdom after Steve's mother passes as well and Steve is forced to be a servant to him for ten years. When Steve finally has a chance to escape, he finds friends in a group of seven iron golems. But Herobrine has other plans and poisons Steve. Knowing the only way to save him is to find his true love, the seven golems embark to find her. Can Steve be awoken in time to reclaim his crown and take over as the rightful ruler of the Overworld? Find out now inside!

Alice and the Ruby Queen Squared

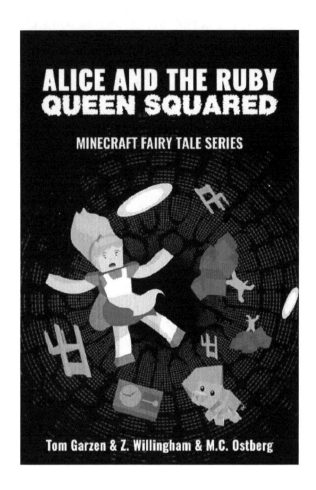

Alice is an ordinary girl in an ordinary world when one day she sees a square pig and follows it down a dark, deep hole. Now, I know this story sounds familiar, but it is anything but! When she lands, she finds she is in world full of blocks. Everything is square - including her. After meeting with a strange man named Mad Cap, she is told she was brought here to save the Overworld from the evil Queen Ruby. She is given specific items that will help her on her quest. Armed with a magic cake and drink. Alice ventures into this new world and picks up some friends along the way. Using her magic items, as well as her trusty bow and arrows, she makes her way into the world of Minecraft. Will Alice be able to defeat Queen Ruby and still make it home safe? Find out now inside!

Peter and the Skeleton Pirate

PETER AND THE SKELETON PIRATE

MINECRAFT FAIRY TALES SERIES

Tom Garzan, Brayden Bush & Z. Willingham

Peter and Tink are on their way home from a party at the Darling house when Tink nods off. With Peter left to navigate the way home and the sun quickly rising, there is sure to be an issue. Seeing four stars instead of two, Peter picks the wrong one and ends up sending them spiraling into a vortex of the unknown. What happens next includes a skeleton pirate, some really dirty socks, a bunch of large metal beats, a dainty burp and a group of determined villagers. Will Peter and Tink be able to help save the day AND make it back to Neverland?

Hoody and the Cave Endermen

Hoody is an Enderman with a conscience. No longer enjoying stealing from the villagers, he tries to stand up to his fellow Endermen - only to be kicked out in the cold. Zaq is a young boy with a keen eye and knows something is happening with the village items that keep getting stolen. After a day in the woods, he comes across an Enderman who seems different. The two of them soon become the best of friends and team up together to help save the village from more thefts and to stop the evil Endermen from coming back. They have a plan, but can they really trap and all the Endermen and save the village? Find out now inside!

Alex is a girl who loves walking through the woods, kicking skeleton butt (or bones) and especially visiting her grandmother. But things have been changing in her little village. People are starting to act... strange. So she goes to check on her grandmother one day, wearing her thick red cloak against the cold. What she finds is something of her worst fears. Her grandmother is not the same as she used to be! Steve is a wizard who is down on his luck. No one will buy his potions and he is starting to doubt his abilities as a healer. Knowing of the zombie changes in the local villages, he has set out to make a potion that will cure those afflicted. The problem is he has no one to test it on. Will Alex, her grandmother and Steve find a way to cure all of their problems? Find out now inside!

Skelur and the Golden-Tipped Arrow

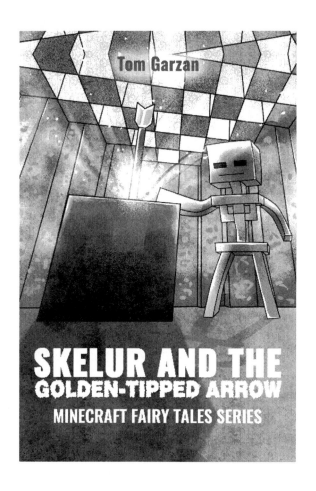

Skelur is a small, skinny skeleton with a big skull

that gets picked on by everyone and is never

allowed to go on raids. King Bonerot has tasked

him with finding new villages to raid for

food. After being given a mysterious prophecy by

the Grand Elder, Skelur sets out on a journey that

will change his life and the lives of all the

skeletons in his village. Go along in this epic quest

inside now!

Daisy and the Creeper Beast

Creepy is a cursed creeper, but he will never tell you

what he is cursed with. He is so lonely. So when he

finds a man trying to take one of his precious blue

flowers, he wants nothing more than for him to stay

with him and be his friend. But the man is afraid and

Creepy isn't the best at convincing people to be his

friend. Demanding he send him his daughter, he lets

the man go.

Daisy is a girl unlike any other. Beloved by all,

especially her father. She would do anything to make

him happy and keep him safe. So when he is

threatened by a creeper, she sacrifices herself by going

to live in a scary castle deep in the woods.

Will Daisy survive the dangers that lurk in the castle?

And will Creepy ever find the friend he so wants and

cure his curse?

34050610R00053

Made in the USA
Middletown, DE
06 August 2016